good deed rain

We passed a streetsweeper on the boulevard and we picked up water on our wheels. I could see Morning Star in the mirror. We were almost there. Someone in a yellow vest swept the cement on the corner. Between the skyscrapers of hotels and offices, blue sky was slowly being painted.

This is
the author's 58th book.
Others include: *Home Recordings,
Lake Erie Submarine, Homeless Sutra,
Go with the Flow, Pinocchio in America,
The Puttering Marvel,*
and many more…

the
AIR
OVER

PARIS

"In 16th century England, chairs were rare articles of furniture. Commoners sat on stools or benches."

 —*History of Endowed Positions*, USC School of Cinematic Arts

"I don't know what a chair is, but Jack Oakie deserves a table, too."

 —Red Buttons, USC School of Cinematic Arts dedication, 2003

The AIR OVER PARIS

Allen Frost

Good Deed Rain ◊ Bellingham, Washington ◊ 2023

Mr. Twit was a twit. He was born a twit. And now
at the age of sixty, he was a bigger twit than ever.

—Roald Dahl

INTRODUCTION

We left our son in California and returned to a colder, rainier place. The house was a lot emptier. I started searching for a Roald Dahl book to distract me. I knew it was somewhere. I opened cupboards and went through boxes and looked under beds and I was still thinking about Rustle in Los Angeles. This book is set there. We spent three nights on 8th Street, two stores away from Paris Bagels. I took notes while we were there and started writing a book when we got home. This is the Hollywood movie.

the chapters....

What year is it? 2042. I know that sounds futuristic, but I assure you, 2042 isn't that different. In the morning two suns rise and I go to work, I unlock the padlock gate and we're open for business. Blanc and Bumps. Semi-Sentient Speedbumps for Hire.

My Martian friends are awake already, lights blink along their sides, their version of good morning. In baking terms, you could say the bump resembles a croissant, until it's laid across the road, then it looks like a baguette. I wave on my way to the tractor.

We have a busy day, Paris Bagels wants us there by eight, so I need to hurry. Getting a bump into the trailer takes a bit of effort—imagine a wrangler back in the day, or a zookeeper prodding a hippo from its bed in the hay. Of course a bump is different than a horse or any creature in a zoo. I have three on the lot, they're each a little different in temperament. For the Paris job, Morning Star will be perfect. I can rely on her to be still, to slow the traffic on 8th which is usually quite plentiful and loud. I'm not exactly sure how aware a semi-sentient speedbump is. Nobody, even those who handle them, entirely understands what we're dealing with. I've heard stories where a bump will turn on its handler—suddenly you're flat as flypaper—but I've never had much trouble. Maybe because I treat them alright. They're my friends. I don't use a whip or a long-handled spar.

Morning Star shuffled when she felt my approach. They don't make sounds, other than that of their movement, communication relies on those lights that shine on their sides like portholes. The neon lights rippled along her thick hide. There are a lot of ways they blink, somehow I'm sure a language is going on, but it's no more knowable than a whale's. Morning Star is a good forty feet long, gray as cement, gentle as a trained elephant. I patted her and she followed me onto the trailer, folding herself to keep from overflowing. "That's good," I said.

Once she was aboard the trailer, I shut the gate. Her parents twinkled goodbye, they knew the routine, they knew I'd be back in a while for one of them too. On a busy day, it would be the whole flock.

With a tin rattle, the tractor engine started and we were on our way. So long to the lot on Flower Street, the tall fence trimmed with razor ribbon, graffiti on the gateway. Cosmic Reward lifted his head to watch us leave. Or maybe it was his other end.

Paris Bagels is my favorite place in the world. They've been our most loyal customer and I guess you could say more than that. We know the way there, I bet we could get there blindfolded.

We would have to be quick getting Morning Star stretched across the street. There's a fine art to this kind of work. I had to tape patches in place to block the other lights on Morning Star so she would only blink PARIS. Someday maybe I can use a typewriter to tell a bump what to spell.

As soon as PARIS began to flash, the cars, the wagons and carts had to slow down and pull over for that word on the road. They couldn't help themselves, all they could think of would be a morning coffee and baguette. Human nature doesn't change. P.T. Barnum used to draw them in with elephants, all I need is a semi-sentient speedbump.

2.
ODETTE

Odette was waiting for me at the curb. Knowing I was on the way, she had blocked off a parking spot for our arrival. The bakery opened early, she started making bread by candlelight, the shop was watched over by melting wax, and I swear I was guided there by that glow and the scent in the air.

We passed a streetsweeper on the boulevard and we picked up water on our wheels. I could see Morning Star in the mirror. We were almost there. Someone in a yellow vest swept the cement on the corner. Between the skyscrapers of hotels and offices, blue sky was slowly being painted. We scared pigeons off the road, splashing to either side a clockwork racket of wings.

Odette waved. She had flour on her arms and apron. I steered for the blue neon PARIS sign and there was plenty of room to park.

I leaned from the wheel. "Hi, Odette."

She said good morning. We've known each other for a while. Oh, it's not romantic, I have no time for that, believe me. Who has time for love? These bumps keep me busy running around, and her French allure is just a flower to me. Picture Humphrey Bogart saying that as he makes the foggy run to Martinique.

She pushed through the slats of the trailer and told the Martian creature something I couldn't hear. Maybe it knew what she said, a few lights rippled across its back like a purr. Maybe those two could have carried on a conversation, the first of its kind between an Earthling and a bump, but I didn't have time to wonder, I had to lead Morning Star onto the street.

As I've already explained, there remains a lot of mystery about these creatures from Mars. We know enough to make use of them for our simple needs and that's about all.

I made a racket unlatching the tethers. Odette took a step back towards the café, out of my way. She was busy too, the bakery would be open soon. She told me to come in for a coffee when I was done and I said thanks, I would.

I dragged the ramp down and Morning Star knew what to do. Our scientists have assured us that bumps are not much different than a starfish—they react to the current around them and hang to the ground as long as they have what they need. Commanding them is easy, that's what they say, and I have found it to be true.

A last car rolled by and with the street clear I tapped Morning Star and she slid across the road from curb to curb. I didn't have to remind Morning Star what came next. She was already blinking PARIS, PARIS, PARIS…

A bicycle neared. The rider slowed, braked, and as she rolled over the bump she glanced at me and it took all her skill not to crash land. She left her bike against the post office box and ran for Paris Bagels. One thing I've noticed, once a bump begins to work, nobody can resist the lure. It's like the Martian projects a sort of hypnotic power. Those were the people Paris Bagels fished for. The city was a sea that was filled with them. Truthfully, it was working on me too. Now that I was done, I was ready for Odette's coffee.

caught on film

3.
TATI

When I returned to Flowers Street, I stopped the tractor at the gate, got out and took off the padlock and rolled open the wide chain-link. I drove through and parked. I was a little surprised there was no sign of the other bumps. Usually they're out there in the open. They could have sought shade around the other side of the shop. A siren hurried on the boulevard on the other side of the yard. I've heard stories of bump rustlers, that's why I keep the gate padlocked. I also have a security robot with a camera on the premises. He would have been alerting me if there was danger. Everything had to be okay, I could hear him playing accordion somewhere nearby. He stays busy. When he's making his movies, if anyone trespassed they would surely be caught on film.

Something didn't seem right though. The

bumps were not lying in the shade around the corner. I never had one escape, where could they go? They'd be hard to miss on our streets. There was nowhere else they could be. "Tati!" I yelled.

The accordion stopped. "Up here!" He was up on the slanted roof, right on the edge, his legs and feet dangling over the gutter. He held his accordion on his lap, with a tripod next to him, camera pointed straight up at the sky.

"What are you doing, Tati? Where are the bumps?"

"See for yourself," he said.

I turned and looked at the cloudless blue sky.

Two perfectly round balloon-like spheres dotted the air. They were a little smaller than pennies, gaining distance and height above the city.

"They can fly!" Tati cheered and he began to play music again.

"Since when? They can't!" I couldn't believe my eyes. "We need to get them down! I have another job to do!" But they were way beyond my reach or the sound of my voice. What was I supposed to do? They just seemed to be drifting on the breeze. How do you catch a lost balloon?

Or two?

"Wait there," I told Tati. "I have to make a phone call. Keep an eye on them." I knew he would. Tati was in his element, making his next movie.

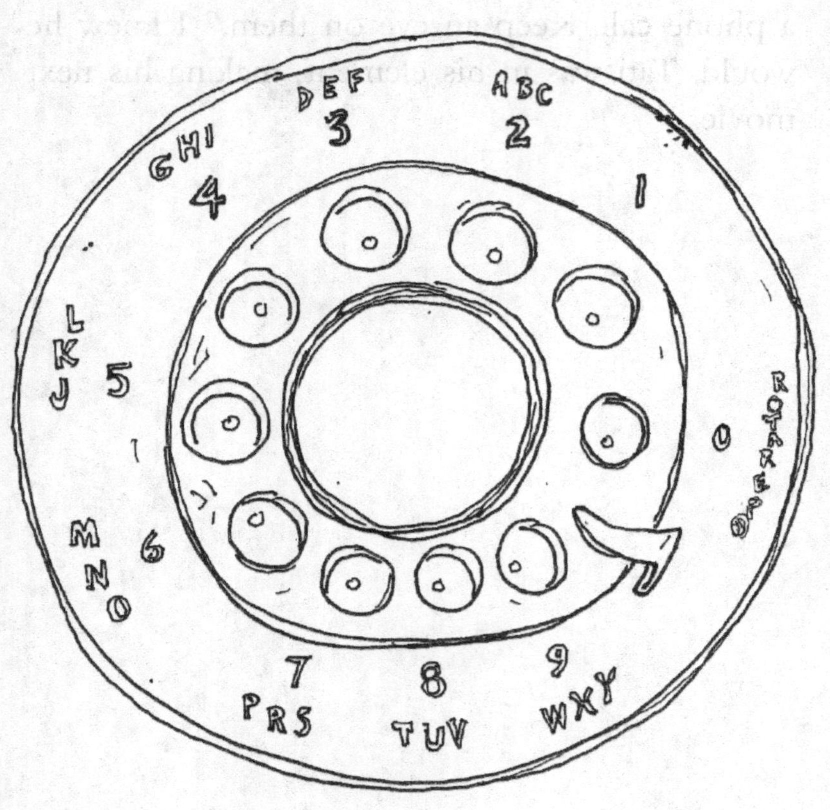

a babbling lunatic

4.
TRAFFIC DIVERSIONS

It was cool inside my office. The air-conditioner hummed. I went to my desk and pushed aside folders and papers to get to the telephone. I picked up the receiver and started to dial. It isn't a number I often call, but I have it memorized, most of the city does I bet, it's on billboards and jingles on the radio airwaves.

"Good morning. La Plume Traffic Diversions, Renée speaking. Can I help you?"

"Yes, can I speak with Mr. La Plume?"

"I'm sorry, Mr. La Plume is—"

"It's very important, Renée." I explained who I was, where I worked and how I had a situation with two bumps that was new to me and I thought it would interest them too and I'm sure I sounded like a babbling lunatic.

"I'm sorry to hear that, Mr. Blanc," she told

me. "But Mr. La Plume is in Des Moines today, at a dealership conference. If it would help, I can transfer you to one of our handlers."

"Sure. Thank you." I carried the phone to the window and peered out the venetian blinds.

I saw bent aerials and chimneys and fence posts spun with barbed wire.

"This is Pierre," a gruff voice greeted my ear.

"Hello, are you the bump handler?"

"One of them."

Of course. A place like Traffic Diversions would have an entire crew of handlers. I explained how two of my speedbumps were currently flying over the city.

He said, "Impossible."

"I assure you I'm telling the truth. There's no mention in the owner's manual of such a thing but it's happening and I need some assistance."

"Hold on a moment," the handler said. A lot of noise wrestled in the background, shouts and slamming doors and breaking glass. I heard an electric crackling zap of the whips I would never use on a bump. Then silence.

"Hello?" I waited and repeated, "Hello?"

In another moment, Renée's voice returned.

26

"Mr. Blanc? Are you still there?"

"I'm here. What's going on there?"

"The bumps! It's just like you said, they're inflating and floating away. I can't believe it! I'm watching all of them fly off the lot!" Someone near her screamed and the line went dead.

I appreciated the quiet of my office after that. It wasn't for long though. I had to go back into the shining hot suns and see what the air had in store.

5.
A JOB on EARTH

It's been a while since astronauts set foot on Mars and discovered life there. They were quick to catalog all the varieties, animal, vegetable, and mineral, to figure out a use for them and what could be adapted to our society back on the home planet. Vern La Plume was one of the hundreds of entrepreneurs who explored Mars and he returned with a rocket full of bumps. He was the first one to discover their ability. He exploited that peculiar behavior for his business venture on Earth. Why use them as speedbumps? It seems crazy but that's how he made his fortune.

I went to Mars with him on his final collecting trip. I thought it would be like that Melville novel. He was Ahab and I was Ishmael. Outer space as the open sea. We were loaded with rope and nets and tractor beams. Mars isn't much more than dust and rocks and broken pottery. It was much harder to find bumps by then, it was never easy to begin with, but finding one in that vast orange desert had become nearly impossible. We were lucky to find two. They might have been the last bumps on Mars.

I kept them company in the hold on the way home. The metal floor was covered with Martian dust and crushed rock. It comforts them. I still keep a layer in my yard at work. Not many people would go to such trouble, ordering fifty-pound bags of Martian Crush, certainly not La Plume. He chains his semi-sentient bumps in rows on the hot tar lot of Traffic Diversions.

Our rocket had trouble on the return trip. We ran into a meteor storm. The main power supply was knocked out for a week. We floated in outer space. The bumps didn't like it. I did my best for them, but by the time we reached Earth they were in sorry shape. Vern took one look at them on the landing pad and gave the ladder a kick. He was furious—here he was, taking a rocket to Mars and back for nothing. Then he surprised me. It was like the end of the Charles Dickens book after Scrooge has been haunted by ghosts all night.

He told me to take the two useless bumps. They were as good as dead, he said. If I could revive them he told me I could keep them, I could start my own speedbump shop, he didn't care. Vern La Plume was the one who discovered the speedbumps, he's considered the last word on them. Anyone in this business is just following in his footsteps. La Plume Traffic Diversions has a big lot on Fig Street where they must have fifty or more bumps parked in rows. He wasn't worried about a smalltime operator with two deathly speedbumps. He kicked the ladder one more time before he turned and left.

It all happened at the right time. I was ready to find a job on Earth and settle down for good. Cosmic Reward and Double Indemnity recovered. We started Blanc and Bumps at 3994 Flower Street. I even got a card made:

Melville Blanc
Humanely-Treated, Range-Free
Reliable Martian Bumps for Hire

The first year was rough, as I guess it is for most businesses. Paris Bagels saved us. Honestly.

The day I met Odette I knew she was extraordinary. And I've seen the perfect Martian earthrise when our planet comes into view. She wanted to know all about how I went to Mars and what happened next. I asked her about Jean-Luc Godard and Anna Karina. We had coffee and watched the traffic on 8th. She's great, she's one of a kind. Like I said before, Paris Bagels saved the day. All I mean is that establishment became a regular contributor. Morning Star and I know her street, we can slow everything down for her, so every bicycle and car has to stop at her store. She always asks me to stay for coffee.

Before I opened the office door, blasting myself with daylight, I returned to the telephone. I wanted to call Odette. I only needed to make sure Morning Star was still there. As I reached for the phone it began to ring. Funny that happens sometimes, I'll be thinking of Odette and she will call me. That's just an ordinary phenomenon, an everyday psychic connection.

It wasn't her though. It was Claude Berringer. Claude is an accountant at Traffic Diversions. I hear from him every year at tax time. La Plume Industries still counts Double Indemnity and

Cosmic Reward as dependents. Berringer's usual dry delivery was frantic, twisted like a dishrag.

When I could get a word in, I said, "I don't know what's happening either."

"We lost our entire inventory!" he shrieked.

"Me too," I said.

"What am I going to tell Mr. La Plume?"

I didn't envy poor Berringer. I once saw a furious La Plume bend a golf club around a palm tree. You couldn't tell someone like that the truth. I had been to Mars with him, I had seen him squeeze every shadow on the red planet until he hunted each bump down and stole them all, every last one.

6.
ORBIT

I didn't bother telephoning Odette. I went straight to her. I didn't want her to worry if Morning Star started to float.

There wasn't any room to park in front of Paris—no wonder—there was a line out the door and cars parked up on the curb. I would have to try around the block for parking, maybe even one of those expensive lots. The traffic slowed going over Morning Star—vehicles of all sizes can drive over her toughened hide—and as I steered over just like them I got the same craving for coffee and a buttered roll. Morning Star was functioning perfectly. Even for me it isn't easy to resist. I thought of Odette. I wanted to turn onto the sidewalk and run to her.

At the intersection, I took a left. It looked like a space by the Hotel Calais. In 2042 we still have the same trouble finding parking in the city. Some things are eternal.

A spindly robot was standing at the curbside and took it upon itself to guide my tractor trailer into the spot. It lifted a Renault in front of me and angled it some so my bumper could fit. Then it gave me a signal to cut the engine. It was pleased with itself, you could tell. It marched to my window and said, "Are you here for the chair?"

I didn't falter. You need to be quick in a situation like this, where you just fall into a great parking space. I nodded. "That's right."

"I will let them know you are here."

"Good," I nodded. "I'll get a coffee. I'll be back in a minute."

The robot hurried away into the hotel. I have to say, smart as they make them now, there's a certain joy to savor when you outwit a robot.

There's so much going on in this city, every second, everywhere you look. Up the rows of windows, I checked the sky, but all I saw was blue. My affection for Paris was growing as I crossed Olive Street and got closer. When Morning Star is working, everyone is drawn into the orbit, you can't help it. I've seen people without a dime cup their hands and beg.

I heard a helicopter and wondered if it was chasing after the speedbumps. Without them, Traffic Diversions was done. I was lucky I still had an earthbound one. Paris, Paris, Paris, it called me.

7.

The ONLY WORKING SEMI-SENTIENT SPEEDBUMP in TOWN

An abandoned police car had dammed the road into one lane to allow for parking on the street. The blue and red lights were flaring, the door was left open. The officer was inside the café with the crowd. Pandemonium. All I had to do was take Morning Star away and this scene would return to an ordinary day. But I couldn't do that. Business was booming.

La Plume would be strategic with his speedbumps. He would plot the city map like a battlefield, placing Martians here and there wherever they would draw the most attention. I never had that attitude. I try to help out the little storefronts, the horse-carts and bodegas and one time a blind man selling pencils. I guess that's why La Plume was never worried about my competition.

With the only working semi-sentient speedbump in town, the effect was powerful, it was like an undertow. I was pulled along the sidewalk. It took all my strength to fight my way past the door. I couldn't have got in anyway, I never saw so many customers, they steamed the windows, they filled the café like a beehive.

It was too much. I knew it. I had to admit it. Against the tide, I plodded off the curb into the street. I crushed a paper cup with my heavy shoe. I had to climb between two jammed cars to get to Morning Star. A kid's scooter and a bicycle were tangled on top. Someone's sneaker was left behind.

"Morning Star," I said, "I have to turn the volume down."

A green light blinked.

I dropped my hand and felt along the hard Martian skin. The fiery glow of the flashing message began to soften. I found it easier to breathe. I'm sure everyone else did too.

"Thanks," I said. With Morning Star on the lowest setting, West 8th Street could become itself again. I patted Morning Star. Even though they're supposed to be only semi-sentient, I talk to them.

I feel sure they know what we're saying. "Thanks for sticking around too. You probably know that Cosmic Reward and Double Indemnity flew away. I don't know where they're going. Do you?"

Before I got an answer, a car blasted its horn behind me. Traffic was starting to move again and I was kneeling in the middle of the road, talking to a speedbump. I waved at the driver, "Okay!" I grabbed the bike and the scooter off the street on my way and set them against the lamppost on the sidewalk.

The frenzy at Paris Bagels had calmed. Now that Morning Star's frequency was dimmed, the café wasn't the magnet it was. Except for me. I stopped at the window. Through the crowd I could see the counter. Odette caught my eye and waved. She motioned for me to stay put as she made her way to the door.

She looked like she had been around the world this morning. She looked alright though.

"Hi," I said. "How are things in Paris?"

"Melville…You have no idea! There's nothing left! They bought everything and I have a stack of orders for tomorrow."

"Busy, huh?"

She fanned her face with her hand and sighed. I didn't want to keep her long, I could tell she just wanted to collapse on a chair. I told her I came back to check on Morning Star. I didn't tell her about all the other bumps in town taking off for who knows where. I didn't want to start another commotion. I asked her if she was done with Morning Star. I thought maybe I'd load up the trailer and go back to the ranch. I'd like to keep an eye on the world's last semi-sentient speedbump.

a tall wooden throne

8.
The KING of CLOWNS

Do you know I've daydreamed about Odette. What would it be like with her…would we go to the movies and walk by the aqueduct the way lovers do? Would we go to cafés and the seashore and trails in the woods? She was on my mind as I returned to my tractor.

From a distance, I couldn't help but see the trailer had a new occupant. The Calais robot wasn't about, but I remembered it promising me a chair. And sure enough, there it was. What a sight…

It dawned on me that the sly robot pulled one over on me. I should have known better than to try and outwit a computerized brain. The things you do for a parking spot! The shabby chair that was now tied down to my trailer looked like it was made for the king of clowns. A tall wooden throne painted gold with tattered and patched red embroidered cushions. It didn't improve as I got closer. The robot didn't leave me with a lemon, I got the whole fruit tree. A nimbus of moths made a halo over it.

"Oh, come on!" I grumbled. I looked around. Where was that mischievous robot? This wasn't fair.

The chair didn't think so either. It let me know. "This is an outrage!" it declared. "Do you realize that I've presided in the Calais for nearly a century, a faithful servant, and this is my reward. Dumped on the street like a vagrant who can't pay the rent. Where next for me? The Bastille? The guillotine?"

I felt the burn of robot eyes, as if it was hiding nearby, watching and laughing. It probably did this all day, this was probably its job, emptying ballast from the Hotel Calais.

"Listen," I said, "I'm sorry you feel this way, but I'm not in the market for a chair. In fact, I need the trailer space for my speedbump. I'm sorry to do this, but I'll have to put you on the sidewalk, that robot will have to bring you back to the hotel." I tried to lift it and winced. "I don't know how I can get you down——what do you weigh?"

"I beg your pardon?"

"I don't think I can manage anyway, not unless I tip you out. I wonder if there's a pawnshop around here?"

It gasped, "A pawnshop? At the very least, you should bring me to a museum. I happen to be royalty."

"Really?" That much I had guessed. "Well, I'm not going to stand here arguing with a chair. I have to get out of here before that robot drops more unwanted furniture on me. I guess I'm stuck with you. I'll take you home. You'll have to make room though."

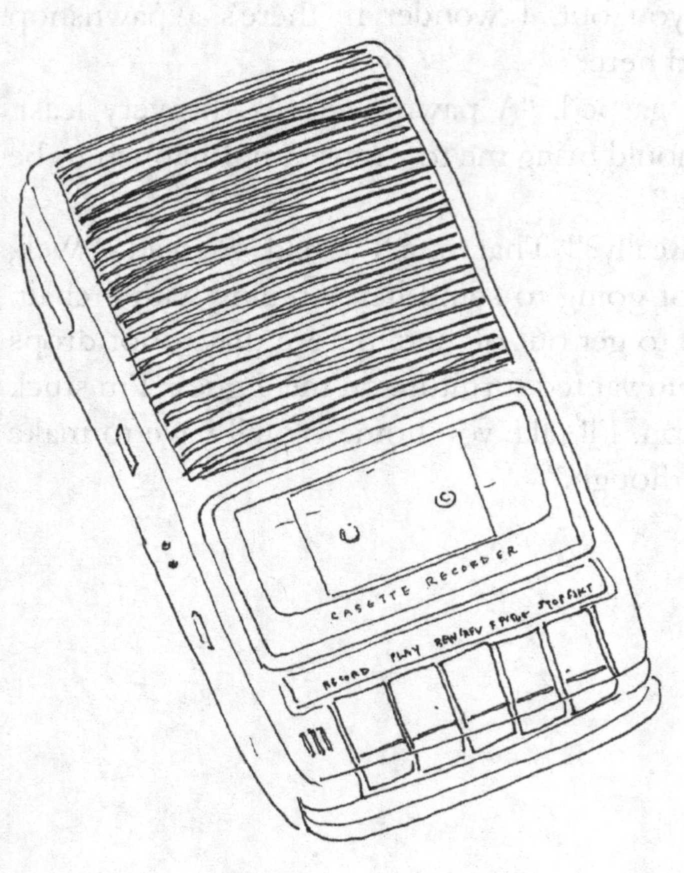

taped to the bakery

9.
The MAGNETIC FIELD

I settled myself on the tractor seat and started the motor and circled the block, turning onto 8th from Hill Street and driving slowly over the bump to stop in front of Paris. I switched the hazard lights on and hopped out. A sign was taped to the bakery door, FERMÉE. Not bad, I thought. Well done, Morning Star. But there must be something else a bump can do with all that power. Why does everything have to be about making money? That was all that mattered to La Plume and now his fortune had gone up in smoke. Or at least up a half mile over the boulevard.

The chair said something as I circled the paneling, unlatched the tailgate and dropped the ramp. I didn't want to get stuck talking with it. Tati would, I bet. He could fill a whole movie with Charlemagne's voice. I swatted a chain out of the way. I made enough noise I didn't have to answer the chair. I could ignore it for now but I suppose I'm stuck with it, at least for a while. I'm a little surprised nobody at the Hotel Calais dismantled the spindle that lets it talk. How could a hundred years could go by at the hotel and nobody thought to do that? "I'll be right back," I told it. I started to whistle something that wasn't a song until I was out of range.

Morning Star stretched across the street. Lights dazzled around the word PARIS. I entered the magnetic field. I pictured Odette holding a bagel. Once the speedbump was safely stowed on the trailer, I promised myself I would go say hi. The compulsion was like walking against the tide, with your feet catching the pouring sand. The traffic squeezed past me, bunched to one lane, but nobody seemed to mind, such was the calming emanation coming from the Martian creature signaling warm thoughts.

I greeted her and she knew I was saying it was time to go and that's usually all I need to do. This time, she didn't move. "Come on, Morning Star." I don't know if she fell asleep, sometimes they turn dormant, but they always wake for me. Still, this was a strange day for bumps, something was going on. I repeated her name and clapped my hands. I never had this trouble before.

"Is she alright?" Odette asked. She had appeared on the road near me and kneeled with me all powdery from the bakery.

"I'm not sure."

Then we both read the message on her as it changed. The new word in lights was UP.

I glanced at Odette and she tilted her head, hand raised to shade the suns. There was flour on her neck. "Melville! Look!"

Way overhead, dots formed, a circle in the blue sky. All those missing bumps from La Plume's lot made a floating hoop. Maybe Cosmic Reward and Double Indemnity were with them too, beads in necklace shape.

Bumps in the air over Paris, a talking chair, words spelled in Martian light, it was just another day in 2042.

10.

LEARNING FRENCH

"What are they doing?" I asked Morning Star.

The spots of light on her turned into a new word. RETURN, followed by another, MARS. I got it now, they were all leaving our planet. A helicopter was circling them. I don't blame them for wanting to go. Who wants to be run over by tires all day?

Another word flashed on the speedbump, READY and that changed to NOW.

"Okay," I said. I stepped back and gave her room. Her ends rolled up, turning her into a ball. It was like letting go of a balloon watching her skim the graffiti wall of the Hotel Bristol. I knew this was the end of Blanc and Bumps. I was glad she waited long enough for me to say goodbye.

We didn't get long, Odette and I, watching her. Suddenly there was no reason for the traffic to be

48

slow, everyone was in a rush to get somewhere else and they let me know it. A city bus steam whistle, cars veering in the other lane honking horns, even the bicycles with their rattling bells.

Odette and I ran back around the trailer and hopped into the tractor cab. No more semi-sentient speedbump and it was like water breaking through the dam. I started the engine and we lurched ahead.

Neither one of us could speak for blocks until somewhere past the Orpheum. Odette laughed, "What am I doing? I jumped in here with you so fast I wasn't even thinking!"

We both laughed. She looked behind us, out the window, over the top of the chair, searching the sky dancing with tall buildings and palm trees. "I don't see them anymore. They must have gone to Mars." She looked at me, "What'll you do?"

I shook my head. "We're almost to the ranch. I promised a chair I would take care of it. If you don't mind. Then I can drive you back."

Odette gave me a funny look. Then she shrugged and reached for the dial on the dashboard and turned the radio on. Only it wasn't a radio station that played, it was the tape deck.

"Je m'appelle Melville."

I reached for the dash, but Odette stopped my hand.

"Where is the sea?" the cassette continued. Then it said in translation, "Ou est la mer?"

Odette turned to me all bright, "Are you learning French?"

Yes, it's true, I've been trying to teach myself since I first met her, but I'm a slow learner. I thought I could surprise her one morning chirping French like a bird. I turned the machine off before it said any more, but it was too late, now she knew.

"Ohhh," she clucked and put her hand on my shoulder and I guess it was good she unwrapped a secret I kept from her.

I asked Odette how long it took her to learn French when she was little, I mean could she remember the discovery of certain words like *orange* and *aviary* for instance, or did she already have other words in mind, did she know a different language before she learned French and did my asking make any sense?

She smiled. She said girls and boys born in France have all the words in them already, like a packet of seeds, or a recipe. She squeezed my shoulder. I think she was kidding me. I'm not sure though, for all I know France is another planet as different as Mars.

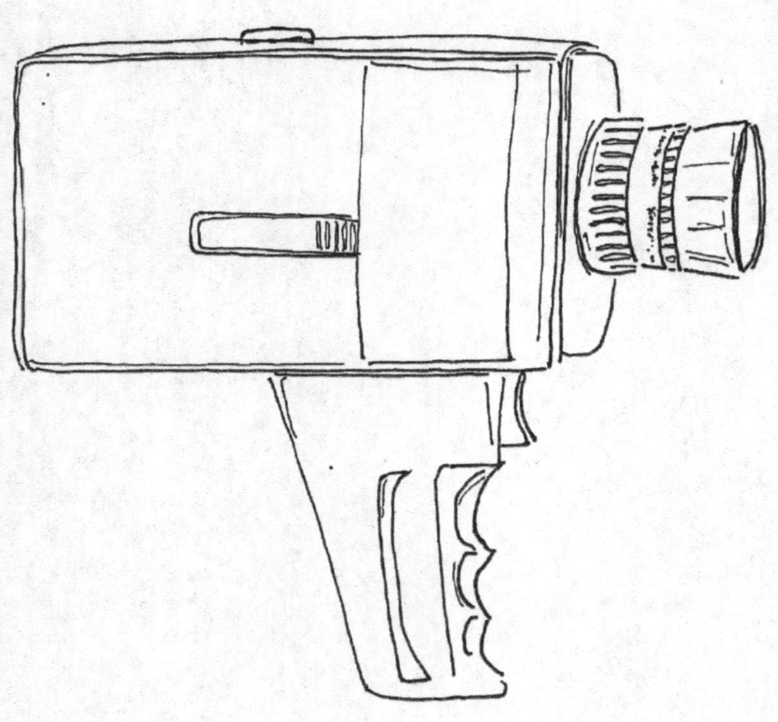

no more Martians to film

11.
The ROBOT LECTURE

We were on Flower Street, getting close, Odette had never seen the ranch before. There wouldn't be much to it now, no Cosmic Reward, Double Indemnity, or Morning Star to come home to.

Tati opened the gate for the tractor. He was probably out of a job too, no more Martians to film. We parked on the red crumbly dust and left the cab.

The chair awaited in the trailer. I figured Tati could help me get it to the ground. After all, it was a robot like him who put that chair up there.

Tati, ever alert, had already noticed our cargo and had his camera before his eye, whirring. I would ask him to help when he was done with the shot—I learned never to interrupt the director. He brought the camera down and asked me,

"Where did you get it?" Before I could explain, he hopped up into the trailer and marveled, "My next question—why did you get it? I didn't think there were any semi-sentient chairs left." Tati bent and peered at it, "Does it still work?"

"Yes," the chair replied in a mouse-like squeak.

Tati found that hilarious, slapping his metal knee. "I can't believe it! What a rare day this is today." He set his camera on the thick red cushion and gave us a chair lecture. It seems there was a brief period of time when semi-sentient furniture had its heyday. A chair like this one was top of the line, it would have been bearing some mogul or sheik, no ordinary elite. It would have been present at council meetings while vast amounts of money exchanged hands. Honestly once Tati got on a roll it was like being in 7th grade and I sort of lost interest, glancing at Odette instead. She listened and nodded while Tati droned on. I was never one for pompous lectures—especially when the subject is chairs—it seemed like our robot commentator would soon be at home sitting on that throne, ordering a thousand shares of stock, delivered to his yacht. I hoped Odette didn't mind being dragged into this. Where did he get the impression that she wanted his attention? I was tempted to pass her a note—*Let's get out of here!*— we could always escape, I could take her hand and we could make a break for it.

"And that," Tati concluded, "is a concise history of the once glorious semi-sentient robotic chair."

"But why would you want a talking chair?" I asked.

Tati said, "Weren't you listening? The chair was considered an advisor, an ally, and also an invaluable accountant when sums were involved." He glared at me, "A robot mind is considerably more adept than a human."

Odette stopped herself from laughing, barely, but it was true. I couldn't think of a comeback, not right away. Years ago, there were standup comedians who were known for their verbal jousts with hecklers. Alas, where are they now?

nothing to guard anymore

12.
The ROBOT'S LATEST MOVIE

I opened the garage and Tati carried Charlemagne in. That was the chair's name. I guess that figures. Tati set it down in the pale blue light of the window. "This is perfect," he decided.

I must admit I am thankful a robot is strong enough to carry a solid throne like Charlemagne, it must weigh more than a washing machine.

Tati slid the tripod apart and pointed the camera at the semi-sentient chair surrounded by the gloom. Soon the robot would be busy with his latest movie and it wouldn't matter that our livelihood had only just recently floated from our atmosphere. Blanc and Bumps had been separated by a hundred million miles. With nothing to guard anymore, Tati and his security camera might as well film Charlemagne, why not?

Odette and I returned to the yard. It was hot

outside. I wondered if she was ready to go back to Paris but she was curious about my place. So I gave her a tour. I showed her where the three bumps spent their time when they weren't working. The tracks they left in the Martian dust as they slowly roamed were still here. They didn't do much, they didn't need much. I kept the grounds raked, as if their red planet wind blew new patterns each day. Tati played the accordion for them and they liked that. Music is universal. I tried to create the best place for them I could manage. I know they were better cared for here than the bumps at Traffic Diversions. But of course it wasn't enough. Mars called them home.

We stopped beside my Peugeot. I leave my car in the yard because Morning Star liked to gently push it around, the way a kid will do with a toy in a sandbox. I stopped talking too—Odette was a good listener—I only hoped I could tell a story better than my robot, Tati. I didn't want to press my luck though.

"I'm going to miss them," I told Odette. "I hope Double Indemnity and Cosmic Reward are happy on Mars, doing whatever they do. Morning Star has never been there. She was born here, in this yard, this was her home." I stopped talking again, this time because I simply couldn't. I was overwhelmed. Controlling emotion is another thing Tati is better at.

"I've got an idea," Odette said. "If that jalopy still works, I know where we can go."

"Oh, it still works fine," I promised, though it had been a while. The dents and scratches and smoking exhaust didn't stop us from clattering out to the boulevard.

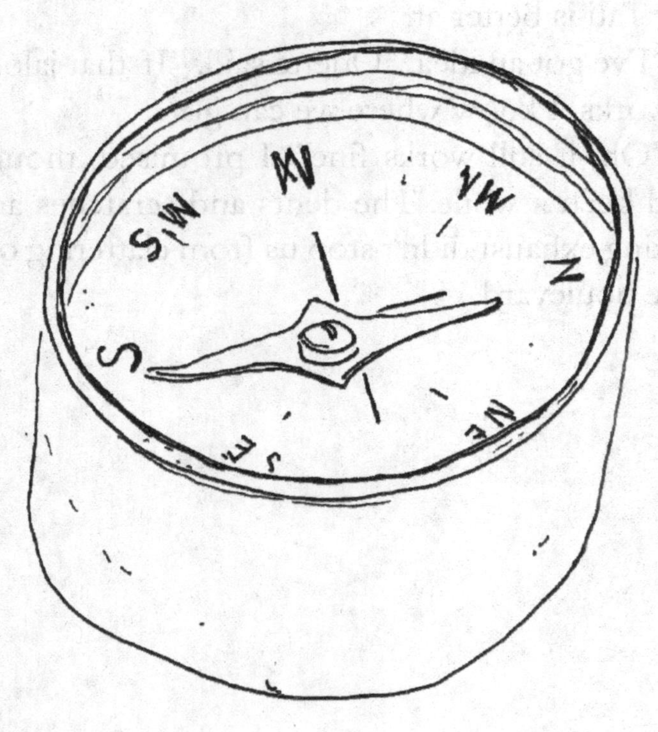

early exploration days

13.
The MARTIAN
NATURAL HISTORY MUSEUM

Odette pointed at the dome rising above the line of trees. "That's the place."

"Really?"

"Yes. It will do you good."

The Martian Natural History Museum wasn't the destination I expected. I haven't been there in years. All the dioramas, displays, and rocket surplus are intense reminders for anyone who's been to Mars, especially of those early exploration days when the planet glowed a quiet orange, before they started to transform its unearthly reality.

Having Odette with me will be nice, maybe I can tell her what I felt.

There's a door on the second floor I know I'll have to avoid. It's an actual rocket ship door and when you stand at it, you can look through the thick quartz window and witness Mars out there as it really looked, so real I can nearly reach for the latch and drop to the ground on the other side.

What good did it do going to Mars? I went there looking for something that now is lost. I would have to find something to replace Blanc and Bumps. Maybe I could work with Tati on his movies. Maybe I could wash dishes in the Paris kitchen. It was overwhelming to worry about. The future could start tomorrow. I parked the Peugeot under a tall eucalyptus tree.

Fortunately Odette didn't intend to go to the second floor—she led me across the shining marble into a dark room—where the walls were lined with windows, each one a frozen life-size scene of the different creatures of Mars. There were Brainees, glowing blue in a cave. If it wasn't for the glass you could reach in. Some students ran past us hurrying to the Camel Bear. We didn't have far to go.

The next display held what came to be known as a semi-sentient speedbump. There were no roads for it though, just the ruins of the canals painted on the back wall of its enclosure. The bump had been built realistically out of vinyl and fiberglass and it even had working lights beaming from its side. I didn't recognize any pattern or words. This idyllic scene was from before Earth contact, so who really knows what they were saying. Probably not PARIS. Behind it, in the near distance, was a herd of more bumps raising red dust. I hoped Morning Star, her parents, and the flock from La Plume were all doing this well—as long as they avoided the settlements and stayed in the deserts and plateaus. I wondered if once in a while Morning Star would think of 8th Street and blink the name of the bakery she used to know.

Next to me, Odette read aloud from the plaque on the window frame. "Collected specimens of this peculiar creature were brought to Earth for study and employment. Although little remains known about its habits and abilities, you may see the Semi-Sentient Speedbump at work on our city streets."

The big vault-like room echoed another tour group coming through. We were quiet. Odette stared at the dream scenery we came here to see. The lights blinked randomly. I watched the softly changing color on her face.

14.
A FUTURE PLAN

I returned Odette to her bakery where there were orders to fill for tomorrow, if the customers remembered to come for them now that the Martian magnetic rays had been unplugged. 8th Street was always busy at this hour with people buzzing from the stores, hotel doors, restaurants, cafés, the Rexall and the grocery. Without Morning Star, Odette told me she expected to lose some business, but she didn't seem worried. Paris Bagels would get the word out the old-fashioned way. I agreed she didn't need help to hypnotize anyone, she already has it all. Tomorrow, while the street cleaners washed and swept the sidewalk, the blue neon light would be shining and the smell of bread and coffee would tumble in the air. I told her I would see her then too, what else did I have to do? Did I have something to fall back on? What did I do before I went to outer space?

I could sign on to another rocket. I bet La Plume was planning a return to Mars, to find the next creature he could cash in on…No, that wasn't for me. I wish Mars had never been found by people like La Plume. I wish it stayed like the paintings in the museum.

I drove home on Broadway where the old movie palaces of the 20th century made me think of Rome. The Orpheum, the RKO, the Mayan, The Tower, The Majestic, The Palace, each one of them once shimmered with neon, covered with jewels of light creating an irresistible effect like fantastic fishing lures that would catch and pull you in. Seducing monuments unrolling dreams inside the dark. Just imagine what that was like a hundred years ago, leaving the sidewalk, going on a journey to the stars. I had to grab the wheel to steer around a man dressed in rags who windmilled in the street.

I don't know what I expected back on Flowers. It would have pleased me to find that Tati and Charlemagne came up with a future plan. Wouldn't that be great? I would be surprised to discover they had.

The Peugeot sputtered to the gate and coughed and gasped while I got out and opened our way into the yard. I would have to take the Blanc and Bumps sign off the chain-link, unless I wanted it to rust there like an antique, like a sign that read *Zeppelin Rides* or *5¢ Ice Cream*.

I parked the car near the garage in the shade. Tati and the chair were talking in the center of the yard by the big potted aloe. I didn't want to interrupt their interview. I quietly shut the driver's door and went to the office.

15.
CHARLEMAGNE

On my desk by the telephone is my calendar book. It seemed only right that I go through the schedule and let my clients know that Blanc and Bumps was no more. I'm sure the whole city has been informed by newspaper and radio and telephone and talk on the street, but in case anyone counting on my business doesn't know about the hovering Martians in the sky, I sat down at my desk and opened the ledger.

It was getting late in the day. I was supposed to have Cosmic Reward at a shop right now… if he was still around…if I hadn't run off with Odette and let time slip away…I picked up the phone and started to call Fishburg Faucet Repair when the office door burst open. I had to shade my eyes from the white suns' light.

A silhouette of a robot stood in the doorway.

I settled the phone back in its cradle. "What is it, Tati?"

"You know I've been making a movie…"

"That figures. Aren't you always making a movie?"

"True." Tati sidled in and shut the door. The air-conditioner set in the window groaned. Anytime that door opened and closed, the warm air rushed into my cool office like a tidepool. "But this is different, this is a documentary, this time I just let Charlemagne tell his story. And let me tell you, that is one fascinating chair."

"Really?"

"Oh yeah." Tati sat on the chair opposite me, not a talking chair, not even semi-sentient, just a plain wooden chair that came with the office. "Do you know he traveled all over before he got marooned at the Hotel Calais."

"Is that so?" I really wasn't in the mood for another chair discussion, obviously I had other things on my mind, not the least of which was what was I going to do with the rest of my life?

"Here's the really interesting part…" Tati leaned closer. "Do you know how he got from point A to point B?"

I shook my head. I could make a guess. From the looks of Charlemagne, I would say he was shoved.

Tati slowly nodded. "Come with me. This is something you need to see to believe."

So I left my calendar and the telephone. Fishburg would have to wait. As I've learned in the past, once Tati gets on a roll, you just had to see him through.

Tati let in the sunlight again, blinding me momentarily. His sensors adjusted to it automatically. He waited for me while I blinked ahead. He watched for my reaction.

Across the red dusty yard, beside the spiked aloe leaves, a shadow was dropped on the ground. Six feet above it, Charlemagne levitated, silent as a ghost.

"Hah!" Tati announced. "Behold! He can fly!"

16.
SPACE SCOUTS

What was going on? Was there a problem with gravity today? Why was everything in my life flying? What was next? Would it be Odette floating past me with the sparrows?

Tati explained, "There's a breaker switch on back of Charlemagne. I moved it from OFF to ON and what do you know, look what he can do!"

The chair stayed perfectly still like a butterfly pinned to the air. There was no sound of a motor or a rotor holding it there. I was baffled. "How does it work?"

"Search me!" said Tati. "They don't make these anymore. Lost technology, like the astrolabe or the Eiffel Tower."

"How do you get a flying chair to land?"

"You just ask." Tati cupped his metal hands and called through the funnel into the air.

"Charlemagne, can you land?"

It was like watching a cartoon where something impossible happens. The big heavy chair let itself carefully out of the sky and rejoined us and questioned Tati, "Did you ask him?"

"No, not yet," Tati said.

I looked expectantly from the chair to the robot.

Tati's speaker crackled and took a deep breath and then said, "We were talking and we had an idea."

"A proposition," the chair added.

What a time for the bell at the gate to ring. I turned around and looked across the yard towards the sound. "Oh no…"

Tati noticed them also. "Space Scouts… Should I tell them to move along?"

"No," I said. "I'll talk to them. But don't you and the chair fly away. I'll be back in a minute."

A girl rang the bell again.

I waved, "Hang on! I'm on my way." I kicked one of the bits of orange Martian gravel ahead of me as I hurried. What idea did Tati and Charlemagne have? What did their combined robot brainpower conceive of? This was like one of those radio serials that ends each week with a cliffhanger. "Has our hero Melville Blanc met his doom, or will a robot and an anti-gravity chair save the day? Find out in the next exciting episode!"

Five Space Scouts gathered on the other side of the gate. They liked ringing the bell. They all took a turn before I got to the gate. I wondered what they were selling. Or were they just trying to get a bell-ringing merit badge?

The tallest one, a girl around eight, got right to the point. "Mister, would you like a box of Martian truffles?"

"No. I'm busy. I'm sorry."

"You can buy one," said a boy.

"Or as many as you like," said another scout.

"No thanks." Presuming we were done, I started to walk away. I wanted to hear about the robots' idea. I only took a couple steps when one of the scouts called after me.

"My dad sells you Martian gravel."

I stopped in my tracks and turned. "Is that right?"

Even though my semi-sentient speedbumps are gone and I have no need for buying more gravel from Mars, I had to be careful. Let's just say his father could make my life very difficult.

The kid sneered at me. "My dad said we could count on you."

I dug into my pocket and took some money. It was enough, it had to be, it was all I had. "Thanks very much," I said. "And tell your father thanks for the gravel."

The gravel kid stuffed the money away and they all cheered and sang out together. I stood there holding the box of truffles until they moved on to the next address on Flowers Street.

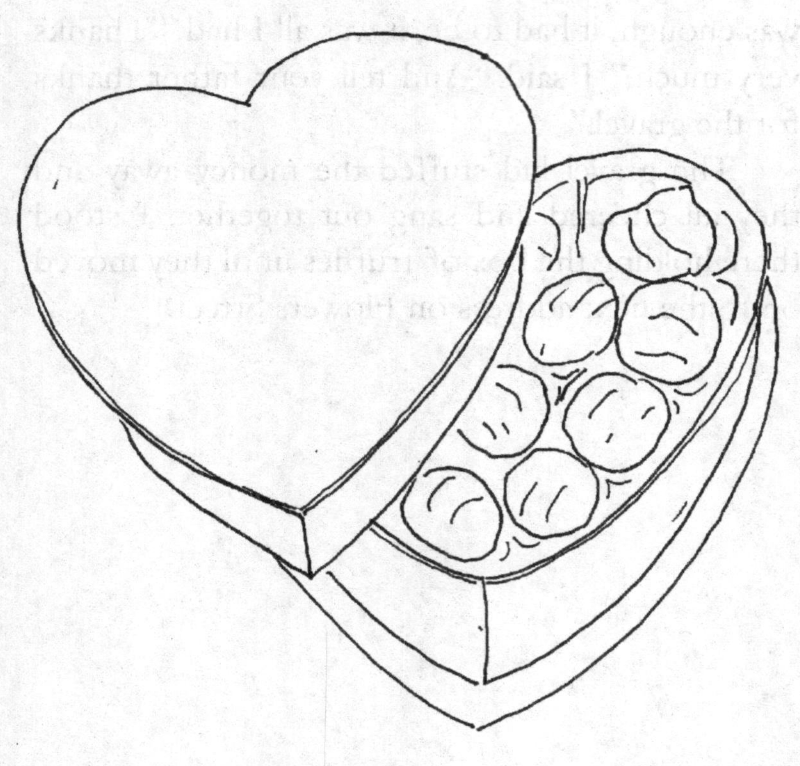

what's this idea?

17.
An AIR of MYSTERY

Tati and Charlemagne were muttering as I returned. I don't know if anyone in the world has ever been more anxious to hear what a chair has to say.

"Oh, look at that!" Tati exclaimed. "You brought chocolates." The film camera zoomed in.

"Yes, well, I sort of had to. There's a Martian mafia in this neighborhood, but you didn't hear that from me." I tucked the box under my arm and knitted my hands together. "So, what's this idea of yours?"

Tati swiveled, "Charlemagne, would you care to explain?"

I listened. At first it seemed like lunacy. The idea of me sitting in a flying chair while it hovered over some business, while I crowed into a megaphone with a banner unrolled and fluttering

75

in the air beneath my dangling feet, a hundred feet up. It sounded dangerous too. I said so, but they insisted, and in the end they convinced me. I didn't need the semi-sentient speedbumps to continue my promotional business. A flying chair would create just as much interest they assured me. In any case, it wouldn't hurt to try.

I didn't expect us to start so soon, they couldn't wait though, they wanted to see what would happen. Tati hurried to the garage to look for banner supplies while I went back to the office to call Fishburg and let him know that something a little different was on the way.

I wanted to go straight to Paris and try the chair there, surprise Odette, but Tati, director of countless movies, observer of life on Earth, had another idea. At first I didn't want to listen—what's a robot know about needing to see someone like Odette? He insisted we had to gain experience, we needed a trial run. I envisioned the Titanic. We'll be in the *Herald*, he said. That's how we develop a following, an air of mystery. He and Charlemagne agreed. I said okay, but then we go to Paris.

It made sense the way they said it. Anyway, it got me to the phone. I dialed and pretty soon I was talking.

"Hello, Mr. Fishburg, how are you? This is Melville Blanc…Yes, I know we're running a little late…No, I'm on my way…Yes, I know it's your store's anniversary today, don't worry I have something special…Well, yes that's true, we won't be using speedbumps anymore…They…Mars… They all went back to Mars…No, it just means that I've had to improvise. I found a solution, something I assure you will captivate not only you and your customers, but the whole city. Fishburg Faucet Repair will be the talk of the town!"

18.
FISHBURG FAUCET REPAIR

I don't know how the pigeons do it, they make it look so easy. Telephone wires, signposts and poles, aerials, trees, radio towers, not to mention all the jagged rooftops. I was tied to the chair with a loop of strong rope, I shouldn't have feared falling out, but it was hard not to. Charlemagne kept to a steady flightpath, high enough above the street, but I held on tight to the arm rests and sometimes I had to close my eyes. "Look out!" I cried again as we missed a tall palm. I had to lift my feet over it. I know it wasn't right of me to question an experienced flying chair, still who knows the last time it flew? Stuck on a carpet in the Hotel Calais all those years it probably had no idea how this century has changed the topography.

As if reading my mind—and maybe it was capable of that, would that surprise anyone?—

Charlemagne said, "My goodness, look at that road!"

"That's the interstate," I said, shutting my eyes again. It's not that I'm afraid of heights, if I was a bird using my own wings to fly, I would feel like I was in control and the sight of ten thousand cars below would just be another river on the landscape.

"So many people now…" the chair marveled.

"We're not far from La Brea Avenue. Do you see it? Do you see Fishburg Faucet Repair?" I could find it in my tractor, but I had no idea what it looked like from the air. I had to fool my eyes to open them. I needed to pretend that I would see a field and Odette would be waving to me in the wildflowers.

Charlemagne said, "There it is!" and he was correct. I recognized the green pagoda roof next door. I used to park in front of China Dragon when I unloaded a speedbump. Fishburg's was a nondescript store until the bump began to hum and blink, then you couldn't help but notice it. The pagoda and anything else in the near vicinity seemed to fade away as you fell into the trance of the faucet repair shop.

I said, "Take us a little lower," and felt us drop like an elevator. "A little slower please…"

We ended up fifty feet above the silver awning and Charlemagne remained stationary, something a chair has a special talent for. "This will do," I said.

The megaphone was looped around my neck so it wouldn't fall as I leaned forward to unveil the banner Tati had twined and rolled tight like a parchment underneath the chair.

With a whoosh, the words rattled down. A red banner, giant letters that spelled: FAUCET REPAIRS 25! The chair moved a little as if the wind caught in an unfurled sail.

Time for the megaphone. My hand was shaking. In our rush, I hadn't prepared a speech. I would have to make it up as I went. I thumbed the switch and spoke into the microphone. "Hello! Hello everyone. I come in peace." Wouldn't you want to know everything was okay if you saw me? I was a strange apparition floating fifty feet above the street. "Have you seen the deals at Fishburg Faucet Repair? Did you know this is their 25th anniversary?" My voice echoed off the walls and was swept about by the cars. I was already running out of things to say. I tried a little background. "Fishburg started working on faucets twenty-five years ago. Where were you that long ago? If you were here at La Brea, you would have witnessed a miracle. Fishburg Faucet Repair was born! How lucky we are! Fishburg brings the world relief. Every house has an annoying drip. Does is keep you awake at night worrying?"

It was exciting, this new job of mine, but I wouldn't say it was an improvement over a semi-sentient speedbump.

19.
LA BREA AVENUE

I had gained a spectator. An audience of one. A man stood on the sidewalk and stared at us. I felt a little better seeing that. One was the start of a crowd. Then he yelled my name and I realized it was Fishburg himself.

"What are you doing up there?" he shouted at me.

"Mr. Fishburg! Here he is everyone! Owner and visionary founder of our fair city's finest faucet repair! Celebrating a quarter century of innovation and spectacular savings. Mr. Fishburg, do you have anything you'd like me to tell the good people?"

"Yeah!" he bellowed. "Get the hell down from there! This ain't no circus!"

"You just need to give it time," I pointed at the passing traffic. "They'll soon be swarming

Fishburg Faucet Repair. Look! Here's someone now!"

A black and white cruiser pulled beside the curb. It was okay, maybe the officer wanted a new sink for the station. The doors opened and two police shaded their eyes staring at me and the chair. "What's going on here?"

"That's what I want to know," Fishburg joined in.

I was still talking through the megaphone. "We're celebrating twenty-five years' service to the community!"

Finally a couple pedestrians walking a dog stopped to take notice. The dog barked at me. Charlemagne and I weren't as quick to draw a crowd as a semi-sentient speedbump, but we were beginning to work our magic.

"Do you have a permit?" the other officer asked me. She had cupped her hands to yell at me.

I rested the megaphone on my lap and let my reply fall to the ground, "No…" Of course I had a permit for Cosmic Reward, Double Indemnity and Morning Star, but it didn't occur to me that I would need one for a chair.

"Come down here, sir."

"I'm sorry. I have to stay above the wires," I called. Charlemagne responded, descending to the safest distance from the powerline. The banner floated closer to the ground. The dog lunged for it on a taut leash. A few other people had also appeared but it was hard to tell if they cared about faucets. Cars on La Brea Avenue were slowing. "I didn't know I needed a permit," I confessed. They didn't like that.

"What if everyone started flying on chairs?"

"Chairs everywhere!"

They had a point. I didn't want that to happen.

I heard Fishburg tell them, "This has nothing to do with me or my store."

The nerve of him!

We were paralyzed in the air. I held onto the armrest and watched as they ticketed the banner. When I pulled it slowly back up to me, I felt like someone who had gone fishing and only caught a shoe.

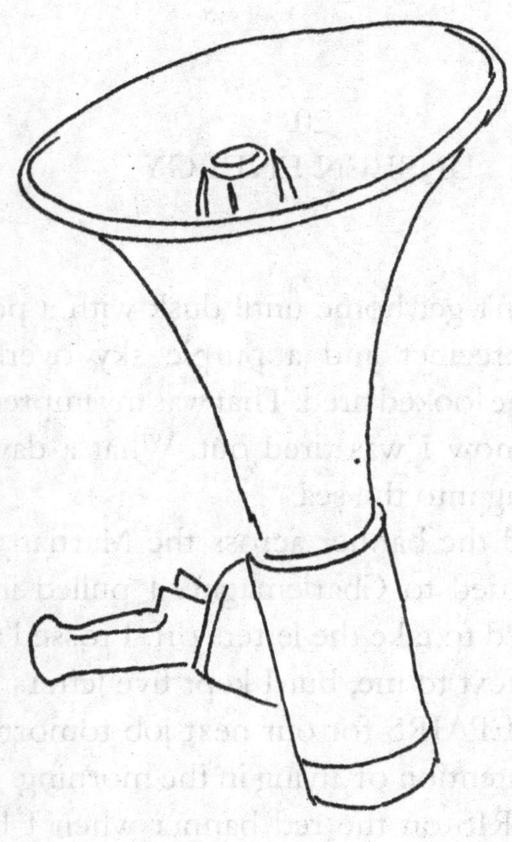

if everyone started flying

20.
UNSEEN ENERGY

We didn't get home until dusk with a permit from the precinct and a purple sky overhead. Charlemagne looked tired. That was my impression anyway. I know I was tired out. What a day was finally setting into the sea.

I pulled the banner across the Martian dust. It was still tied to Charlemagne. I pulled it taut then I started to take the letters off. I tossed them on a stack next to me, but I kept five letters from the word REPAIRS for our next job tomorrow. I had every intention of flying in the morning. I was spelling PARIS on the red banner when I heard the garage door open.

I turned around and laughed. I needed to. Oh, what I had gone through to find that laugh in the form of Tati standing in the doorway. He was wearing a tuxedo. It was so big on him he looked out from it like a battery.

"I know…" Tati admitted, "My suit needs a little alteration. But what do you think?"

"Why are you wearing a tuxedo?"

"Perhaps because my work as one of the leading filmmakers of our time is at long last being recognized."

"What?"

"Tomorrow night," Tati said with a flip of long black sleeve. "I'll be accepting a prestigious award."

That was some surprise. I didn't think anyone but me knew about his movies. I've never even seen one, not completely, and he's been making them for years. I wonder how his appreciation happened. It must be true, there's some unseen energy that lets things happen. Look at me, I'd never be standing here on raked Martian soil, I wouldn't have my own business, strange as it is, I wouldn't have met Odette, I wouldn't even be alive if everything didn't happen just right. Really, it's a miracle.

"How did it go with the fish repair?" Tati asked.

"Faucet repair. Not so good." I told him

about our misadventure. I showed him my permit receipt. Whatever mysterious force it is that rewards us in life must have spent today with Tati instead of me. But I was determined. I told Tati that Charlemagne and I were going to Paris in the morning and this time we would make it work. Somehow.

Tati put his tux on a hanger and helped bring the flying chair into the garage for the night. Sleep was only ten minutes away from me. I felt it sneak up on me like a Martian Dust Weaver, then I didn't feel anything or see any dreams before me. Who knows where I went.

where I went

21.
MAURICE CHEVALIER

I woke from blackness to the sound of Tati's rooster impression.

I'm used to it now but there are still mornings where I'll wake up on a farm, thinking I've got chores to do, animals in the barn, sunrise on the leaves of an oak. I remembered my speedbumps were gone…that hadn't been a dream…they weren't in the yard and Charlemagne was in the garage while a tin robot sat on the eaves crowing at the breaking light of the suns.

"Okay," I groaned. My room is small and dim but some of the blue dawn leaked around the window curtain, reminding me I had work to do this morning. I knew that Paris was already aglow and steaming with good smells. Wouldn't Odette be dazzled when a flying chair appeared above the sidewalk and I'd be floating up there singing her praise for all of the city to hear?

I can recall sunny days a long time ago when there were skywriters. We would stop playing to watch the sky. The dot of an airplane would twist and turn like a spider making a web. Back and forth it would go, the same slow and careful way we would write on blackboards when we had to get in front of the class. Against the blue, a letter would form, chalky as a cloud. It would hang in the air. Then another one would start to form. A word was gradually being spelled out and we would shout what we thought it could be. The little airplane took its time. When it was done, the name of a store or a slogan or logo would have its moment in the sky as the plane buzzed away and the wind up there softly pulled it apart. What a magic spell. I didn't have Martians anymore, but I could do something like that.

When I went into the yard, my robot companions were conferring by the Peugeot. The orange sodium light on the street made silhouettes of them. It was early, the day didn't know if it belonged. The hour when alarm clocks and roosters jumpstart. I carried a cup of coffee towards them.

They must have been awake for a while. They didn't need coffee. Tati didn't bother with a greeting, he spoke like a spinning bicycle wheel, "Charlemagne brought me up to speed, told me everything about the trial run yesterday. I have some suggestions…"

I took a sip of my coffee and noticed the change in the sky. It was already turning a silvery blue. "Go ahead."

"Alright. First of all, you need a script. What's with *coming in peace* and the *visionary founder* and all that?"

I pointed at Charlemagne. "Did he tell you that?"

"I related everything," admitted the chair indignantly, "I have a photographic memory."

Tati nodded. "He told me everything." Patting the chair, he continued, "What you need is a script, something crafted, something that will give you a way with words." He took a book off the hood of the car. "Here, put this in your coat pocket. I marked a page for you to read when we get there."

I said, "We?" Suddenly the chair was getting crowded.

"And there's another thing you're missing…"

Tati reached over the car hood again and lifted his accordion. It wheezed a little like a cat getting picked up. "Music."

His singing wasn't much better than his chicken impression, but neither one could be unheard today.

"You're going to play the accordion while I read poetry?" I asked. I caught a glimpse of the book before I tucked it away.

"That's the plan," said Charlemagne.

"It sounds like a serenade," I said.

The accordion halted and Tati snapped his fingers and winked. "Exactement!"

Oh no, I realized—he's Maurice Chevalier.

22.
GOOD MORNING, PARIS

We flew over junkyards and ironworks, car lots and plots surrounded in barbed wire, zinc rooftops fluttered with our shadow. There's still a lot of poverty in 2042 and then when Charlemagne turned at Broadway Avenue we floated past the Orpheum. I still can't believe that civilization once existed.

Our reflection slid on the office windows and I got a good look. Me, sitting roped to a chair, with a robot playing squeeze-box propped on the backrest, and a long red banner drifting below us that says PARIS. For the first time, I thought maybe this isn't the best idea. But it was too late, the wheels were in motion.

I looked straight ahead. We flowed through a tall canyon of marble, glass, and cement. The traffic crawled below. I held the megaphone on my lap with both hands. There was already so much happening. The chanson sung loud in my ear was the soundtrack of the movie we were in.

I was wondering if this was something I could get used to, soaring over the city like a bird tied to robots. I think I'd prefer just being a bird, with my own wings and all the time in the world to do what I wanted.

"Here we are," said the chair and our motion stopped. This is the part that gets to me, makes me dizzy and want to fall, when I'm stuck in the sky like a neon sign. The accordion wheezed and trilled and Tati launched into a romantic melody. His tuxedo knee bumped me—yes, he was wearing it again, he had tailored it last night so that it fit. I reached in my pocket for the book. This wasn't going to be easy reading a poem into a megaphone. I don't know if they're made for that. I held the book in my left hand, thumbed it open and brought my right hand with the loud contraption close to my mouth.

Tati bumped me with the accordion. He was having difficulty getting comfortable on the narrow backrest of the chair.

I twisted some, but I didn't have a lot of room

either, my rope seatbelt kept me locked in place.

Paris was right below us. Suns' light hit that patch on 8th Street where Morning Star was stretched only yesterday. I couldn't tell if Odette was watching.

I flicked the switch and the megaphone caught my breath. I said, "Good morning, Paris!"

Tati squirmed and hissed, "Stick to the script!"

So I looked at the book and read, "For making the portrait of a bird, first paint a cage with an open door." That was as far as I got. Those were my last words, I had less than a minute to live.

Tati was still trying to get comfortable. His metal foot kicked as he turned to straddle the back of the chair like a horse rider. The poetry flew from my hand. I grabbed his robot foot to keep Tati from falling. The book flapped out of sight, Tati's other foot on the other side of the chair poked the OFF button and that was it. We dropped like a stone. I had time to see Tati open an umbrella and parachute away and then my life was over.

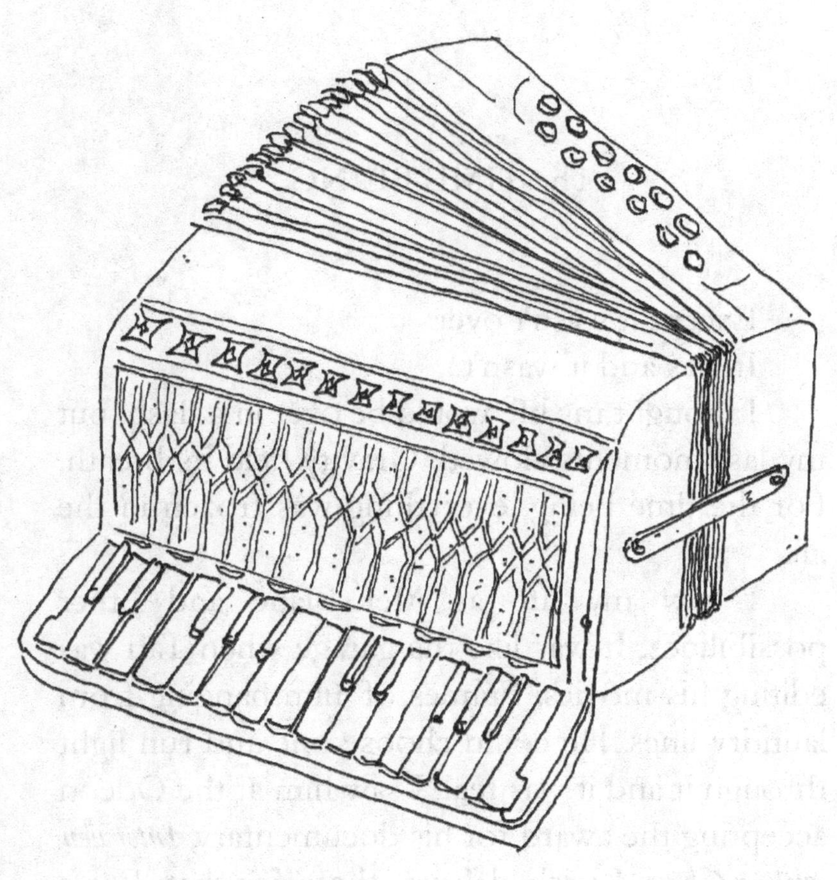

on 8th Street

23.
The TIME BEING

Except it wasn't over.

It was and it wasn't.

I thought my life would be over in a flash, but my last moments slowed. Gravity held its breath. For the time being, everything was frozen in the air.

I saw my life as Mel Blanc and other possibilities. It was like the garage when Tati was editing his movies. Frames of film hanging from laundry lines. He could choose one and run light through it and it was real. I saw him at the Odeon accepting the award for his documentary, *Interview with a Chair*. I wished I was there for that. For a moment I nearly fell into that world. Then I was over 8th Street.

It just occurred to me that I was a bird. I had been one before, I knew what to do. My black wings kept me aloft. I could twist and rise on turbulence. Currents carried me between towers. The feeling made me laugh out loud, what a thrill to be alive and flying a hundred fifty feet from the ground.

Who was thinking this?

What was I?

I was whatever I happened to be.

The city spread for miles below me, full of strange inventions I couldn't begin to understand. It was the flying I was good at. Flying and searching. I'm always looking for something. I don't know what it is, or if I'll ever find it.

Maybe it's that thing in the air bubbled ahead of me.

This was something new. Or was it? I was thinking differently, something was happening to me. Where had I seen that round floating creature before?

You already know, I was only just remembering. The closer I got, I felt it telling me it was okay, "come to me." It wasn't much bigger than one of the things on the street—a car—but it wasn't a machine, it was living like me.

I circled it. I slipped a little and had to flap my

wings. Being a bird wasn't all I was, I was connected to other lives. Not just everything around me, we're part of something further than that—it goes way back and it goes back and forth, forward and back. Now I was a bird, I was also someone else, someone waiting in the air.

I remembered a name and saying it aloud returned me. "Morning Star."

I was sitting in a falling chair and Morning Star was there.

Morning Star had turned around on her way to Mars. She knew this would happen. She steered and shot over Olive Street and caught me and aimed us like escalator stairs towards the ground floor. We went slow enough I saw us in the window of the Atelier Hotel. Lights flashed along her side. I waved at my reflection, sitting like a king.

Just imagine, a semi-sentient speedbump saved my life! I thought about angels. What else could Morning Star be? Below, 8th Street began to move again, out of its sleep, and beside us, I saw the Martian lights in the passing windows become letters. O…D…E…Some words you carry with you from life to life. My cassette lessons call it "déjà vu." A moment of enlightenment. When I put her name together—ODETTE—I almost fell off the chair again.

Hurry, I thought. We're almost there, the Paris bakery, nearly landing on the street, and I know what I'm going to do. Have you ever had your life come to this, where it's crystal clear why you're here? I can't believe I've been given this chance to find my way. Another life is beginning. From this moment on, I won't waste a second of it. I should have done this long ago. All I want is to fly to Paris and knock on her window like the nevermore raven in the poem by Poe.

Finis

The AIR OVER PARIS
Written August 18—September 16, 2022

Books by Good Deed Rain

Saint Lemonade, Allen Frost, 2014. Two novels illustrated by the author in the manner of the old Big Little Books.

Playground, Allen Frost, 2014. Poems collected from seven years of chapbooks.

Roosevelt, Allen Frost, 2015. A Pacific Northwest novel set in July, 1942, when a boy and a girl search for a missing elephant. Illustrated throughout by Fred Sodt.

5 Novels, Allen Frost, 2015. Novels written over five years, featuring circus giants, clockwork animals, detectives and time travelers.

The Sylvan Moore Show, Allen Frost, 2015. A short story omnibus of 193 stories written over 30 years.

Town in a Cloud, Allen Frost, 2015. A three-part book of poetry, written during the Bellingham rainy seasons of fall, winter, and spring.

A Flutter of Birds Passing Through Heaven: A Tribute to Robert Sund, 2016. Edited by Allen Frost and Paul Piper. The story of a legendary Ish River poet & artist.

At the Edge of America, Allen Frost, 2016. Two novels in one book blend time travel in a mythical poetic America.

Lake Erie Submarine, Allen Frost, 2016. A two week vacation in Ohio inspired these poems, illustrated by the author.

and Light, Paul Piper, 2016. Poetry written over three years. Illustrated with watercolors by Penny Piper.

The Book of Ticks, Allen Frost, 2017. A giant collection of 8 mysterious adventures featuring Phil Ticks. Illustrated throughout by Aaron Gunderson.

I Can Only Imagine, Allen Frost, 2017. Five adventures of love and heartbreak dreamed in an imaginary world. Cover & color illustrations by Annabelle Barrett.

The Orphanage of Abandoned Teenagers, Allen Frost, 2017. A fictional guide for teens and their parents. Illustrated by the author.

In the Valley of Mystic Light: An Oral History of the Skagit Valley Arts Scene, 2017. A comprehensive illustrated tribute. Edited by Claire Swedberg & Rita Hupy.

Different Planet, Allen Frost, 2017. Four science fiction adventures: reincarnation, robots, talking animals, outer space and clones. Illustrated by Laura Vasyutynska.

Go with the Flow: A Tribute to Clyde Sanborn, 2018. Edited by Allen Frost. The life and art of a timeless river poet. In beautiful living color!

Homeless Sutra, Allen Frost, 2018. Four stories: Sylvan Moore, a flying monk, a water salesman, and a guardian rabbit.

The Lake Walker, Allen Frost 2018. A little novel set in black and white like one of those old European movies about death and life.

A Hundred Dreams Ago, Allen Frost, 2018. A winter book of poetry and prose. Illustrated by Aaron Gunderson.

Almost Animals, Allen Frost, 2018. A collection of linked stories, thinking about what makes us animals.

The Robotic Age, Allen Frost, 2018. A vaudeville magician and his faithful robot track down ghosts. Illustrated throughout by Aaron Gunderson.

Kennedy, Allen Frost, 2018. This sequel to *Roosevelt* is a coming-of-age fable set during two weeks in 1962 in a mythical Kennedyland. Illustrated throughout by Fred Sodt.

Fable, Allen Frost, 2018. There's something going on in this country and I can best relate it in fable: the parable of the rabbits, a bedtime story, and the diary of our trip to Ohio.

Elbows & Knees: Essays & Plays, Allen Frost, 2018. A thrilling collection of writing about some of my favorite subjects, from B-movies to Brautigan.

The Last Paper Stars, Allen Frost 2019. A trip back in time to the 20 year old mind of Frankenstein, and two other worlds of the future.

Walt Amherst is Awake, Allen Frost, 2019. The dreamlife of an office worker. Illustrated throughout by Aaron Gunderson.

When You Smile You Let in Light, Allen Frost, 2019. An atomic love story written by a 23 year old.

Pinocchio in America, Allen Frost, 2019. After 82 years buried underground, Pinocchio returns to life behind a car repair shop in America.

Taking Her Sides on Immortality, Robert Huff, 2019. The long awaited poetry collection from a local, nationally renowned master of words.

Florida, Allen Frost, 2019. Three days in Florida turned into a book of sunshine inspired stories.

Blue Anthem Wailing, Allen Frost, 2019. My first novel written in college is an apocalyptic, Old Testament race through American shadows while Amelia Earhart flies overhead.

The Welfare Office, Allen Frost, 2019. The animals go in and out of the office, leaving these stories as footprints.

Island Air, Allen Frost, 2019. A detective novel featuring haiku, a lost library book and streetsongs.

Imaginary Someone, Allen Frost, 2020. A fictional memoir featuring 45 years of inspirations and obstacles in the life of a writer.

Violet of the Silent Movies, Allen Frost, 2020. A collection of starry-eyed short story poems, illustrated by the author.

The Tin Can Telephone, Allen Frost, 2020. A childhood memory novel set in 1975 Seattle, illustrated by author.

Heaven Crayon, Allen Frost, 2020. How the author's first book *Ohio Trio* would look if printed as a Big Little Book. Illustrated by the author.

Old Salt, Allen Frost, 2020. Authors of a fake novel get chased by tigers. Illustrations by the author.

A Field of Cabbages, Allen Frost, 2020. The sequel to *The Robotic Age* finds our heroes in a race against time to save Sunny Jim's ghost. Illustrated by Aaron Gunderson.

River Road, Allen Frost, 2020. A paperboy delivers the news to a ghost town. Illustrated by the author.

The Puttering Marvel, Allen Frost, 2021. Eleven short stories with illustrations by the author.

Something Bright, Allen Frost, 2021. 106 short story poems walking with you from winter into spring. Illustrated by the author.

The Trillium Witch, Allen Frost, 2021. A detective novel about witches in the Pacific Northwest rain. Illustrated by the author.

Cosmonaut, Allen Frost, 2021. Yuri Gagarin's rocket lands in America. Midnight jazz, folk music, mystery and sorcery. Illustrated by the author.

Thriftstore Madonna, Allen Frost, 2021. 124 summer story poems. Illustrated by the author.

Half a Giraffe, Allen Frost, 2021. A magical novel about a counterfeiter and his unusual, beloved pet. Illustrated by the author.

Lexington Brown & The Pond Projector, Allen Frost, 2022. An underwater invention takes three friends through time. Illustrated by Aaron Gunderson.

The Robert Huck Museum, Allen Frost, 2022. The artist's life story told in photographs, woodcuts, paintings, prints and drawings.

Mrs. Magnusson & Friends, Allen Frost, 2022. A collection of 13 stories featuring mystery and ginkgo leaves.

Magic Island, Allen Frost, 2022. There's a memory machine in this magical novel that takes us to college.

A Red Leaf Boat, Allen Frost, 2022. Inspired by Japan, this book of 142 poems is the result of walking in autumn.

Forest & Field, Allen Frost, 2022. 117 forest and field recordings made during the summer months, ending with a lullaby.

The Wires and Circuits of Earth, Allen Frost, 2022. 11 stories from a train station pulp magazine.

The Air Over Paris, Allen Frost, 2023. This novel reveals the truth about semi-sentient speedbumps from Mars.

Books by Bottom Dog Press

Ohio Trio, Allen Frost, 2001. Three short novels written in magic fields and small towns of Ohio. Reprinted as *Heaven Crayon* in 2020.

Bowl of Water, Allen Frost, 2004. Poetry. From the glass factory to when you wake up.

Another Life, Allen Frost, 2007. Poetry. From the last Ohio morning to the early bird.

Home Recordings, Allen Frost, 2009. Poetry. Dream machinery, filming Caruso, benign time travel.

The Mermaid Translation, Allen Frost, 2010. A bathysphere novel with Philip Marlowe.

Selected Correspondence of Kenneth Patchen, Edited by Larry Smith and Allen Frost, 2012. Amazing artist letters.

The Wonderful Stupid Man, Allen Frost, 2012. Short stories go from Aristotle's first Car to the $500 dollar fool.

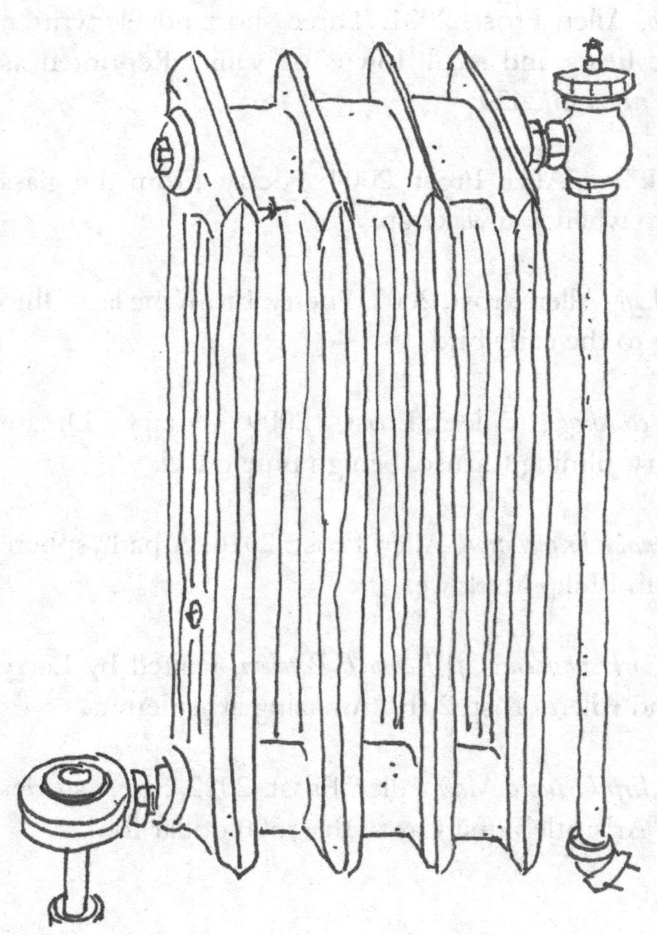